*For Peter
and Lisa*
M.W.

———

*For Lewis
and Thomas*
B.F.

First published 2005 by Walker Books Ltd
87 Vauxhall Walk, London SE11 5HJ

2 4 6 8 10 9 7 5 3 1

Text © 2005 Martin Waddell
Illustrations © 2005 Barbara Firth

The right of Martin Waddell and Barbara Firth
to be identified as author and illustrator respectively
of this work has been asserted by them in accordance
with the Copyright, Designs and Patents Act 1988

This book has been typeset in Columbus

Printed in China

British Library Cataloguing in Publication Data:
a catalogue record for this book
is available from the British Library

ISBN 0-7445-8663-1

www.walkerbooks.co.uk

WALKER BOOKS
AND SUBSIDIARIES
LONDON · BOSTON · SYDNEY · AUCKLAND

Sleep Tight, Little Bear

Martin Waddell

illustrated by Barbara Firth

Once there were two bears,

Big Bear and Little Bear.

Big Bear is the big bear,

and Little Bear is the little bear.

One day Little Bear went out to play

when Big Bear was busy.

Little Bear climbed up the rocks
above the Bear Cave. There was a place
there, little-bear-sized or just a bit bigger.
"I could have my own bear cave in here!"
thought Little Bear. "With a bed
and a table and a chair."

"Little Bear!" called Big Bear,

looking out of the Bear Cave.

"Little Bear! Little Bear!"

called Big Bear, coming out of the cave.

"LITTLE BEAR!"

called Big Bear, but he couldn't

see Little Bear.

"I'm up here, Big Bear!"

called Little Bear.

"I've made my own cave!"

Big Bear climbed up the rocks

above the Bear Cave,

and Little Bear showed

Big Bear his cave.

"That's my bear chair and my table,

and this is my bed," Little Bear said.

"It's a good cave," said Big Bear.

"I need lots more things,"

Little Bear said.

Big Bear helped Little Bear

carry things up the rocks to the cave.

Little Bear played

all day in his cave.

Little Bear swept

his cave.

Little Bear read

his book.

Little Bear made

his bed.

Little Bear jumped

on his bed.

"Suppertime, Little Bear!"

called Big Bear.

"Could I have my supper up here?" Little Bear asked.

"Well…" said Big Bear.

"*Please*, Big Bear?" Little Bear said.

"Well … all right, Little Bear,"

said Big Bear.

And Little Bear had his supper

in his own little cave.

Then it was bedtime.

"Can I sleep up here?" Little Bear asked.

"All right, Little Bear," said Big Bear,

and he tucked Little Bear up in bed.

"Sleep tight, Little Bear," said Big Bear.

"I'll be in the Bear Cave if you need me."

Big Bear plodded all the way back

to the Bear Cave alone,

without Little Bear.

Little Bear sat up in bed and looked round.

"I'm a big bear in a cave of my own,"

Little Bear told himself.

Little Bear looked out of his cave at the moon

shining through the dark trees.

"Big Bear might be lonely without me,"

thought Little Bear.

Little Bear climbed out of bed.

"I wonder if Big Bear's missing me,"

Little Bear said to himself.

And he went to see Big Bear.

"You forgot to read me

my story, Big Bear," Little Bear said,

climbing up on the Bear Chair.

"I'll read to you now," said Big Bear.

"Did you miss me, Big Bear?" Little Bear said.

"I missed you a lot, Little Bear," said Big Bear.

"I could stay here tonight so that you

won't be lonely, Big Bear,"

Little Bear said.

"I'd like that a lot, Little Bear,"

said Big Bear.

And Big Bear read Little Bear

the Bear Book by the light of the fire.

Big Bear sat in the Bear Chair

with his arms close around Little Bear,

till the logs on the fire had burned low.

"Sleep tight, Little Bear,"

whispered Big Bear.

But Little Bear

was already …

asleep.